P9-DDS-292

When I Care about Others

WRITTEN BY

Cornelia Maude Spelman

ILLUSTRATED BY

Kathy Parkinson

Albert Whitman & Company

Morton Grove, Illinois

For Venerable Thich Nhat Hanh. — C. M. S.

For Parker, with love. — K. P.

Books by Cornelia Maude Spelman
After Charlotte's Mom Died ~ Mama and Daddy Bear's Divorce
Your Body Belongs to You

The Way I Feel Books:
When I Care about Others ~ When I Feel Angry ~ When I Feel Good about Myself
When I Feel Jealous ~ When I Feel Sad ~ When I Feel Scared ~ When I Miss You

Please visit Cornelia at her web site: www.corneliaspelman.com.

Library of Congress Cataloging–in–Publication Data

Spelman, Cornelia Maude.
When I care about others / Cornelia Maude Spelman ; illustrated by Kathy Parkinson.
p. cm. — (The way I feel)
Summary: A little bear explains that he cares about the feelings
of others and that others care about him.
ISBN 0–8075–8889–X (hardcover)   ISBN 0–8075–8898–9 (paperback)
[1. Caring — Fiction. 2. Sympathy — Fiction. 3. Bears — Fiction.]
I. Parkinson, Kathy, ill. II. Title. III. Series.
PZ7.S74727 Wg 2002 [E] — dc21 001004090

Text copyright © 2002 by Cornelia Maude Spelman.
Illustrations copyright © 2002 by Kathy Parkinson.
Published in 2002 by Albert Whitman & Company,
6340 Oakton Street, Morton Grove, Illinois 60053–2723.
www.albertwhitman.com.
Published simultaneously in Canada by Fitzhenry & Whiteside, Markham, Ontario.
All rights reserved. No part of this book may be reproduced or transmitted in any form
or by any means, electronic or mechanical, including photocopying,
recording, or by any information storage and retrieval system,
without permission in writing from the publisher.
Printed in China.
10 9 8 7 6 5 4 3

Note to Parents and Teachers

Caring about others is essential for a healthy society. It reflects our belief that every person is valuable. It also brings us feelings of satisfaction and happiness.

To care about others, children must first experience being cared for. Having their own needs recognized and met provides children with the basis for recognizing and meeting the needs of others.

As they become aware that others feel what they themselves would feel, children learn to respond to people who are hurt or in need of kind attention. We can help children to imagine how they would feel in a particular situation, and to imagine how someone else might feel. Then we can point out that because they don't like to be teased, they must not tease; because they don't like to be pushed, they should not push. (We cannot remain uninvolved when children tease, bully, or are unkind or violent toward others, but need to promptly intervene and make it clear that such behavior is not permitted.)

Similarly, children can understand that because they feel good when others are friendly, they need to be friendly. They can learn that their pleasure in being included means they need to include others.

Teaching compassion is an ongoing, daily lesson as we model compassionate behavior for our children. Seeing their parents and caregivers demonstrate caring for others beyond the family— neighbors, friends, and the wider society—teaches children the value of caring about all people.

Cornelia Maude Spelman, A.C.S.W., L.C.S.W.

When I'm hurt, somebody cares.

Somebody cares
when I'm sick.

When I'm sad, somebody helps me feel better.
I need others to care about me.

Others need me, too.
When someone is hurt, I feel bad.

I care when someone is sick.

When someone is sad, I help him feel better.

I care about others!

Others have the same feelings I have.
I don't like to be teased, so I don't tease.

I don't push because I don't like to be pushed.

I am friendly because I like it when
someone is friendly to me.

When someone shares with me, it feels good,

so I share, too.

I say nice things because I'm happy when
someone says nice things to me.

I try to help others. I feel glad when I can help.

I can imagine how others feel,

and I treat others the way I want
them to treat me.

I care about others, and others care about me!

Promoting Empathy

* Help children name their feelings and talk about them. ("I see that you look upset. Can you tell me what you're feeling?") Serve as a role model by learning to name and talk about your own feelings. ("I feel sad about that, too.")

* When children express a feeling, listen attentively. Don't tell them they shouldn't feel that way. (If a child is angry, you can accept the angry feeling while still limiting the acting out of it.)

* Use stories and books to illustrate others' feelings. ("What is this character feeling? How can you tell? Have you ever felt like that? What made you feel better? What do you think this character needs to feel better?")

* Help children recall instances from real life when they felt scared, sad, lonely, or hurt. Encourage them to think about the actions others took that comforted them.

* Show children that they can demonstrate their caring by being friendly, listening, sharing, or enlisting an adult's help.

* Have children act out with puppets or in role play how others might feel in certain situations. ("What is it like to come to school the first day? How does it feel when someone takes your place in line?") Point out that even though we are all different, we all have the same basic needs and feelings.

* Demonstrate the relief and pleasure we feel when we are able to help others. ("I'm so glad your headache is better now.")

* Have children think of examples from their daily lives that illustrate how we respond to others' needs. ("Our neighbor likes it when we visit her and bring her groceries because she can't go to the store.")

* Talk about how we help others in the larger world. ("What do we do to help people who are sick or hungry, or to help everyone when there is an emergency?") Point out all the ways in which our society shows it cares about others, such as by providing soup kitchens, hospitals, clothing banks, etc. Perhaps children can visit one of these places or see ambulances or fire trucks and talk to the people who staff them.